This book belongs to:

. . . . . . . . . . . . . . . . . .

# Vive la différence!

This paperback edition first published in 2018 by Andersen Press Ltd.
First published in Great Britain in 1978 by Andersen Press Ltd.,
20 Vauxhall Bridge Road, London, SW1V 2SA, UK
Vijverlaan 48, 3062 HL Rotterdam, Nederland
Copyright © David McKee, 1978.
The right of David McKee to be identified as the author and illustrator of this work has been asserted by him in
accordance with the Copyright, Designs and Patents Act, 1988. All rights reserved.
Colour separated in Switzerland by Photolitho AG, Zürich. Printed and bound in China.

1   3   5   7   9   10   8   6   4   2

British Library Cataloguing in Publication Data available.

ISBN: 978 1 78344 661 2

# TUSK TUSK

## David McKee

Andersen Press

Once, all the elephants in the world were black

or white. They loved all creatures,

but they hated each other,

and each kept to his own side of the jungle.

One day the black elephants decided
to kill all the white elephants,

and the white ones decided to kill all the black.

The peace-loving elephants from each side
went to live deep in the darkest jungle.

They were never seen again.

A battle began.

It went on...

and on, and on...

until all the elephants were dead.

For years no elephants were seen in the world.

Then, one day, the grandchildren of the peace-loving

elephants came out of the jungle. They were grey.

Since then the elephants have lived in peace.

But recently the little ears and the big ears

have been giving each other strange looks.

"This book was one of my favourites as a kid,
I simply relished in the gloriousness of a load of elephants
battling it out in a bizarre forest. It wasn't until I was a bit
older that I recognised the importance of the morality
that lay (not so subtly) underneath."

OLIVER JEFFERS